ON the EDGE

and Other Stories

Collins

Contents

Unit 1: Refer to Code planning.

Unit 2

    Core: Crater.............................. 6

    Challenge: An Amazing Food Trip 20

Unit 3

    Core: On the Edge 34

    Challenge: A Strange Place for a Holiday? 48

Crater

Written by Chris Bradford

Illustrated by Jake Hill

Jake had waited all year for this trip. He was visiting a crater. And not just any crater. This one contained a lava pool!

Jake's dad parked the car and got out. Jake joined him by the map as his nan put on her trainers.

The morning sun lit up the crater's rim.

"Get a move on, Mum!" complained Dad.

But Nan was distracted. "Where are the rest of the holidaymakers?" she asked.

"We're late. They would've started off by now," said Dad. "If we stay on the main path, we'll be OK."

Jake started jogging up the track.

"Wait for us!" called Nan.

But Jake couldn't wait any longer!

The path was baked hard and made up of layers of black ash. It crunched underfoot. Jake felt the strain in his legs as the track became steeper.

Jake's dad and nan had to march fast to catch up with him.

Dad mopped his brow as they got to the summit. "That was a major effort!" he said.

They stood on the rim and looked down into the crater. Gases hissed from cracks. Rocks were stained by sulfur. And a big pool of lava boiled at the bottom. It was amazing!

Jake sniffed, then flinched. "It smells like rotten eggs!"

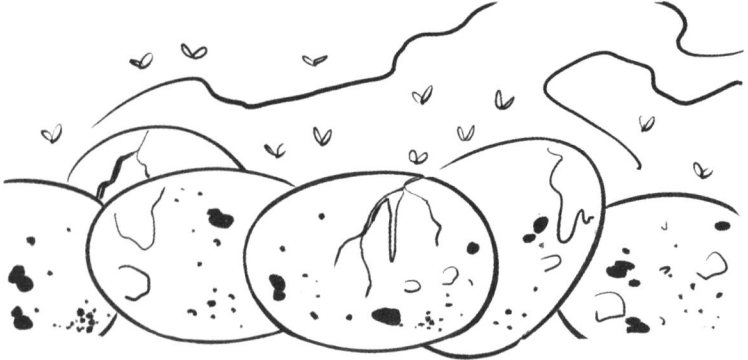

"I still don't see any people," Nan frowned. "This doesn't feel safe –"

"They must be hidden by the mist," explained Dad. "They'll appear soon."

They made their way down to the lava pool. Jake knelt near it and held out a hand.

"Whoa! It's hotter than a cooker!" he exclaimed.

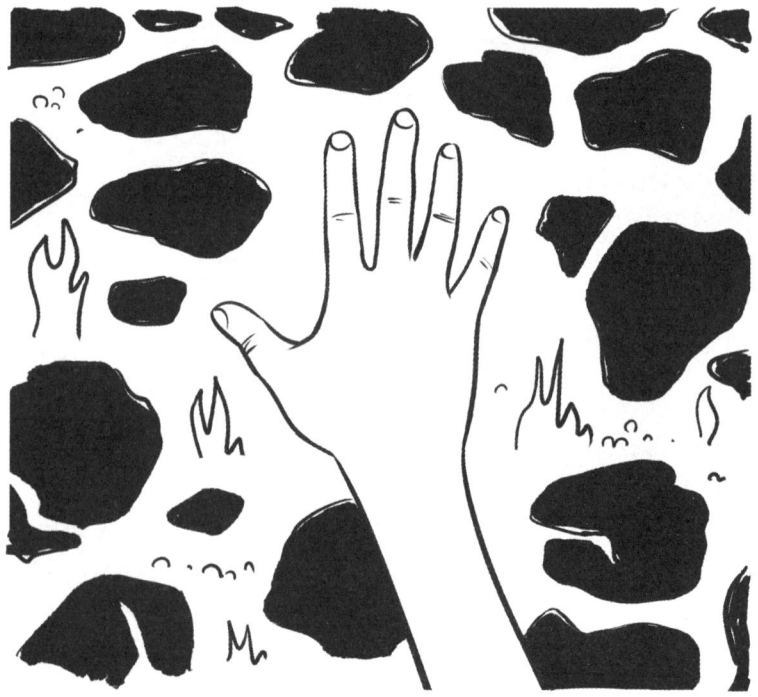

"Don't burn yourself!" said Nan.

"And step back," said Dad. "Slipping in would be fatal!"

Jake stepped away. As they trekked from the pool back to the path, the mist made it difficult to see. They strayed from the path and didn't spot a faded display, which said:

DO NOT ENTER – CRATER IS UNSTABLE.

Soon their way was blocked by rocks.

Jake turned to his dad. "Which way now?"

Dad frowned. "Looks like we made a wrong turn."

Jake felt shaking under his feet. "What was that?" he gasped.

The crater shook again and they could hear a deep rumbling.

Dad looked at Jake in alarm. "I hate to say it, but I have a horrid feeling that the crater is erupting!"

Jake's heart rate shot up as the crater cracked apart … then lava oozed out.

"RUN!" yelled Nan.

They fled the crater. A loose rock made Jake trip and land on his knees. His nan grabbed his arm and helped him up.

The crater boomed and shook again. Jake prayed they would get to somewhere safe soon.

After running down the path for what felt like forever, they made it to the car.

Dad gave a strained laugh. "Well, that's one holiday we'll never forget."

Nan looked like *she* was going to erupt. "Next year, let's just stay by the pool!"

Ash-tonishing facts

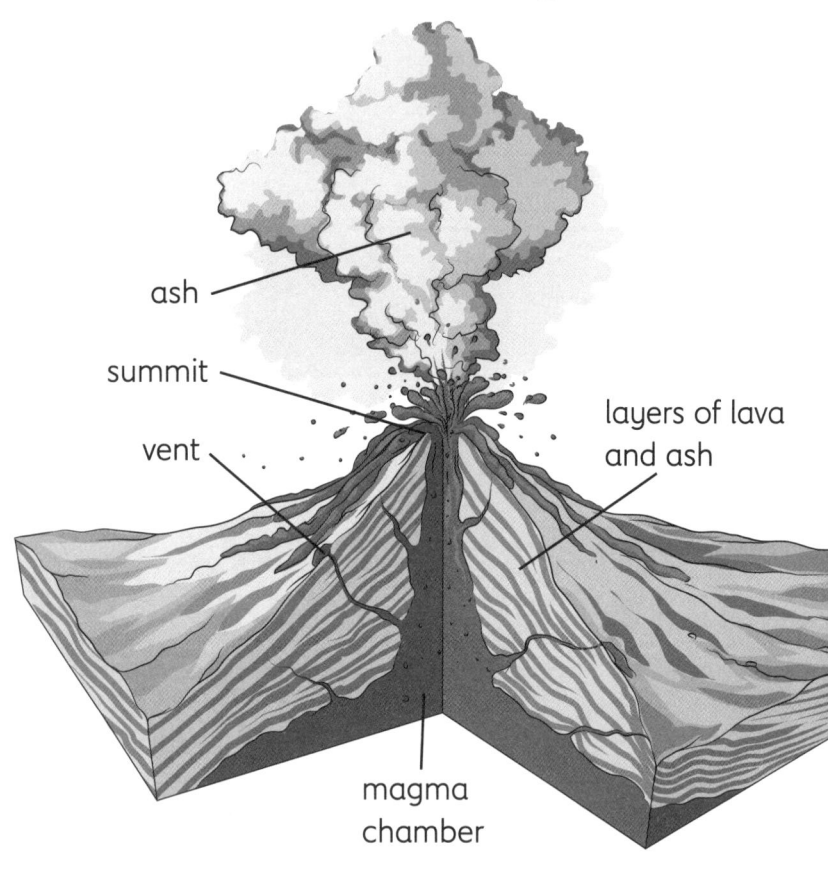

- ash
- summit
- vent
- layers of lava and ash
- magma chamber

Active = erupted within the last 10,000 years; expected to erupt again

Dormant = hasn't erupted in a very long time; may erupt again

Extinct = not expected to erupt again

Spotlight on: Etna

Active, dormant or extinct?:
Active

Fact: 'Etna' translates to 'I burn'

Spotlight on: Three Sisters

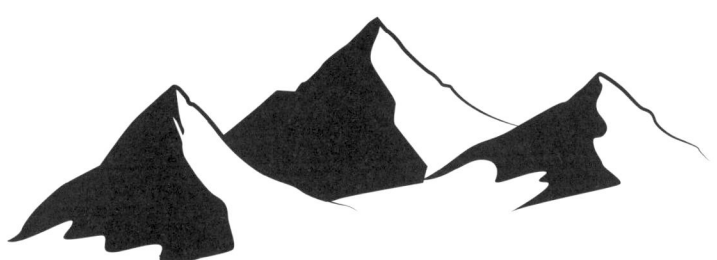

Active, dormant or extinct?:
Dormant (last erupted 2,000 years back)

Fact: The Three Sisters were not formed at the same time, and are made of different rocks

An Amazing Food Trip

Written by Joshua Seigal

Just WAIT until you see the amazing things on display in this trip with a twist!

Your tastebuds will be tested as we take you to see what's on plates across our planet.

You may never look at your food in the same way again. Your morning cornflakes will seem very basic indeed!

A starter in Greenland

Let's start by making our way to freezing Greenland, where people have an interesting way of chasing the chills away …

I present our starter: muktuk.

Muktuk is made with whale skin and blubber, chopped up into little bits. It comes to the table uncooked. The skin is thick, like rubber, but the blubber is much softer. Greenlanders say the skin tastes like hazelnuts.

Muktuk is rich in vitamins and is a food staple for people in Greenland. They freeze the muktuk to preserve it, so they are able to have a filling, high-fat food whenever they need it.

Snacks in Brazil ...

Next, let's pay a visit to a town in Brazil for a little plate of ... queen ants cooked in oil!

We had to plan our trip well as these ants are on sale for a limited number of weeks – when it rains a lot.

When you crunch into your insect snack, you will taste mint! No, your senses have not betrayed you – these ants do taste a bit like this herb.

... or Mexican nibbles?

Or perhaps you'd prefer something sweeter? Travel north, where you'll be able to nibble on assorted Mexican snacks, such as lollipops with insects in the middle!

After this trip, you'll never think of insects in the same way again.

A main dish in Scotland

Let's take a plane off to Scotland to sample a dish that's famed across the planet: haggis!

Haggis is made of the bits of a sheep that often get chucked away, such as the heart, lungs and liver.

Cooks chop it all up, mix in oats and fat, and stuff it into a casing.

Then they boil it and serve it as a filling dinner!

Cheese in Sardinia ...

People in Sardinia love cheese. That's not odd, right? But in one cheese there are ... lots of little MAGGOTS! Perhaps the maggots make the cheese taste better.

However, this cheese is forbidden in some spots as it can make people unwell. Munching cheese full of maggots might not be such an amazing plan!

Would you be brave enough to taste a bit? Or would you be too frightened?

... or battered butter in Texas?

How would you like an epic chunk of battered butter for pudding? Yes, that's right – a lump of butter, coated in batter, and then cooked in hot oil. It's a bit different from your standard cake, anyway!

What a great taste! But don't have too much or you might need a date with the doctor.

A pick-me-up for the plane

As you get on the plane for your return trip, you could spoil yourself with some fermented herring!

There is a dish from the Baltic, called 'surströmming' (say: *sor-stro-ming*). It comes in a tin and is famed for its very, VERY strong fish stench.

Lift the lid and marvel at the looks from your friends on the plane!

You can update them on the amazing holiday you have been on, sampling some of the interesting food our incredible planet has to offer!

Food trip across the planet!

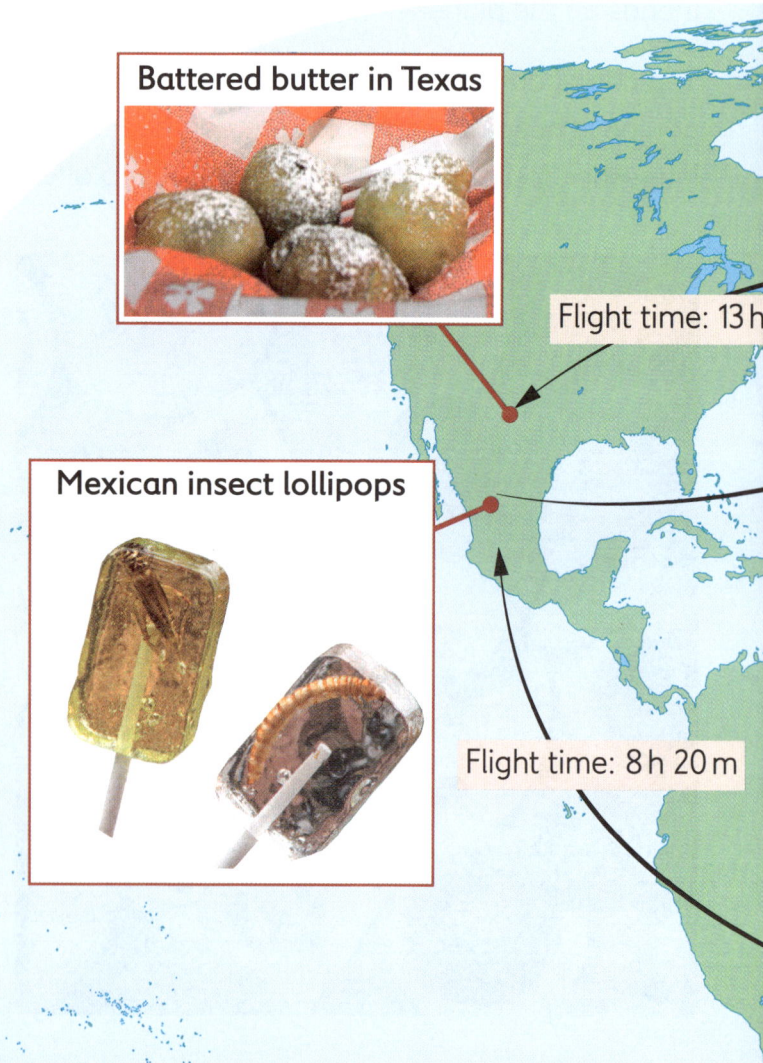

Battered butter in Texas

Mexican insect lollipops

Flight time: 13 h

Flight time: 8 h 20 m

Muktuk in Greenland

Scottish haggis

Flight time: 2 h 50 m

Flight time: 11 h

Maggot cheese in Sardinia

Flight time: 12 h
(but between 24 and
46 h with transfers!)

Ants in Brazil

On the Edge

Written by Samantha Montgomerie

Illustrated by Paula Fernández

"I've booked the best lodge! We set off on Sunday," said Mum.

Grace squinted at the webpage on Mum's tablet.

"Rock and Ridge: A Holiday on the Edge," said Grace, frowning.

"We're staying at the top of the ridge," said Mum.

"Excellent choice!" said Dad.

"Imagine waking up on the edge!" said Grace's sister, Jade.

Grace fidgeted in her chair.

"Getting up to the lodge will be a fun challenge," said Dad.

"But there'll be no signal there!" muttered Grace.

Plus, scaling a rock face would be horrible, she thought.

All week, Grace longed for a last-minute storm to cancel the holiday. But Sunday came and there was not a drop of rain in sight.

No such luck, she sighed, trudging along the footpath.

Mum had pencilled the way on the map. "Here's the ridge!" she said.

"Amazing!" said Jade. She sorted the equipment with Mum and Dad.

Grace's heart fluttered as she eyed the towering rock face.

Mum led the way and scaled up to the ridge.

"Your turn, Grace," she called down.

"You've got this," said Jade, patting Grace on the back.

Grace cringed. Jade loved sports. She'd race up, no problem. But Grace didn't want to budge.

"It'll take me ages to get up there!" she said.

"Just take little, stable steps," said Jade.

OK, I can face this challenge, Grace convinced herself.

She felt for a ledge in the surface of the rock. Engaging her muscles, she pulled herself up.

"You can do it!" called Jade.

Grace grinned. She had started her ascent!

Balancing on the rock, Grace judged the distance of her next step.

She stretched out her hand to grip a flat edge …

… but straining to place her foot, she slipped!

Her arm muscles hurt as she clung on. Panic raced through her.

Grace nudged her foot along, into the surface of the rock. Her legs shook.

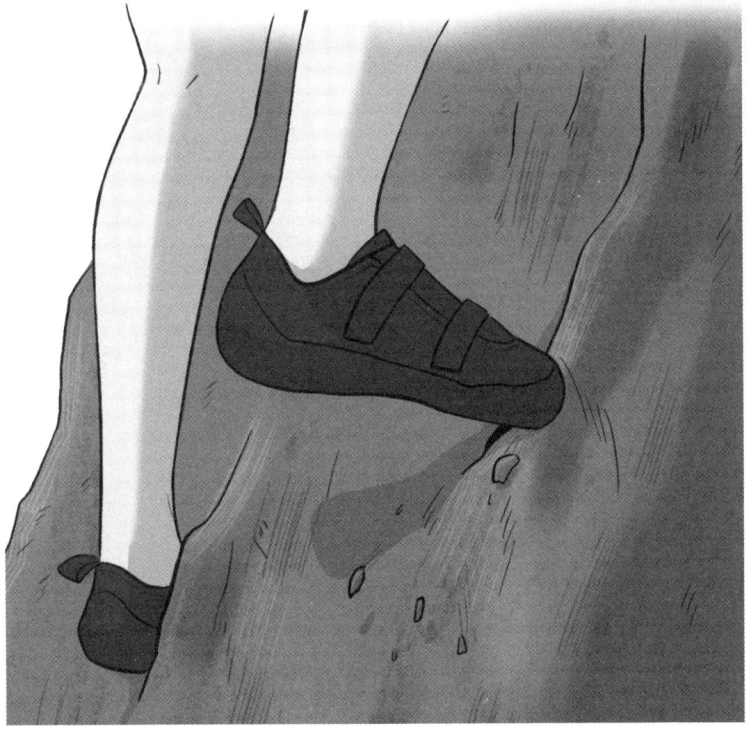

Jade's voice cut through Grace's panic.

"Concentrate. Keep your balance!" said Jade.

I've got this, thought Grace.

With a confident thrust, she pushed off. Then, stretching up, she gripped onto the edge of the rock.

Craning her neck, Grace spotted the top of the ridge. She stretched and pulled, ascending the rock face. She liked the feeling of her muscles at work. She liked the balanced steps and the swing between feet and hands.

It's like a dance, she thought.

At last, she made it to the lodge. "I did it!" she said, celebrating.

"You're a legend!" said Mum, grabbing her fleece. "Now, layer up! I've got cinnamon buns for sunset. Your dad and Jade will join us on the ridge."

Later on, the crescent moon sat like a bright badge pinned onto the velvet darkness of the night. The scent of cinnamon filled the air.

Grace gazed at the stars, scattered like gems.

"I misjudged this place. Holidays on the edge are the best!" she said.

Holiday pictures

@Grace_the_Legend

Just me rocking it at 'Rock and Ridge'

Smashing the ascent!

Celebrating!

Look who took the last cinnamon bun!

Stargazing with Jade

A Strange Place for a Holiday?

Written by Joshua Seigal

There are so many places we can visit – some for a day, some for a holiday! Some people like to visit coastal towns in the UK, such as Margate and Troon. And some prefer resorts in places like Spain and France. But our planet is very big and is filled with a range of amazing places waiting to be explored.

Let's take a look at some fascinating travel spots on offer!

Palau (say: *pa-l-ow*)

If you live in the UK, Palau is very, very far away. It's all the way in the Pacific. Just 18,000 people live there, across 8 inhabited islands. That's not as many citizens as lots of English towns!

In fact, Palau is made up of 340 islands. Boat trips can take you to lots of the islands, but you can't land on all of them.

The unspoiled landscape, coral reefs and lagoons make Palau a tempting place to visit. It might take you ages to get there, but it's a gem of a place for a holiday.

Tashirojima *(Cat Island)*

But perhaps Palau isn't fascinating enough for you. Can I suggest an excellent island that is much stranger?

Tashirojima is an island in Japan that is full of stray cats – hundreds of them! In fact, cats outnumber people.

The island's people claim that the cats bring good luck. The cats are in luck, too, since no dogs are permitted on the island.

There are many Bobtail cats on Tashirojima. These cats have a short, rabbit-like tail. They make good pets as they are gentle and playful.

If you love cats, you're certain to have fun here!

Lake Natron

On the surface, the red, still waters of Lake Natron look gentle enough. Pigments made by organisms in this African lake turn the water red!

But Lake Natron has a hidden danger: a hazard which fools some animals and results in their tragic end. If an animal plunges under the surface of the lake, the toxic waters will kill it!

Images of preserved rock-like animals on the edge of the lake have given it internet fame!

Lake Natron may seem uninhabitable, but some animals and fish manage to live in it.

Very tough leg skin helps!

The lake would be an incredible place to visit – just don't be tempted to swim!

Varosha

If you want a chilling holiday to remember, may I suggest Varosha, in the town of Famagusta? At the beginning of the 1970s, Varosha was a celebrated holiday resort. But it was shut down in 1974, and since then it has been left to decay.

There are large, abandoned tower blocks and streets full of shut-up buildings.

Plants are reclaiming the space and turtles can be seen nesting in the sand.

Cages protect the turtle nests.

Nowadays, you can visit parts of the original resort, but much of it is fenced off and remains off-limits.

Unclaimed Baggage Center

Alabama, US

It's time to pack your bags for your return trip.

Have you ever collected your baggage at an airport and seen some cases that never got picked up? In Alabama, US, you can visit a shop that sells unclaimed luggage!

This shop is a great place to go if you want to see the strange and eccentric things that turn up in lost cases.

Perhaps you will stumble upon that stuffed shark you lost on holiday when you were little. It's your chance to get it back!

Fascinating holiday spots

Unclaimed Baggage Center, Alabama
Average number of visitors per year: 1,000,000
Quick fact: Wedding dresses, sharks' teeth and living snakes have been in stock in this shop!

Lake Natron
Average number of visitors per year: 7,000
Quick fact: The waters of Lake Natron are capable of burning people's skin and eyes!

Varosha
Average number of visitors per year: 700,000 until 1974, and 500,000 after 2020 when people could visit again
Quick fact: Varosha has had no residents since 1974!

Tashirojima (Cat Island)
Average number of visitors per year: 40,000
Quick fact: Tashirojima has between 50 and 80 residents, but hundreds of cats live there!

Palau
Average number of visitors per year: 86,000
Quick fact: Palau is made up of 340 islands but just 8 are inhabited!

Acknowledgements

The publishers gratefully acknowledge the permission granted to reproduce the copyright material in this book. Every effort has been made to trace copyright holders and to obtain their permission for the use of copyright material. The publishers will gladly receive any information enabling them to rectify any error or omission at the first opportunity.

p16 CLOUD-WALKER/Shutterstock, p17t Eugenia Petrovskaya/Shutterstock, p17b Fawad Shakir/Shutterstock, p20l & r AlenKadr/Shutterstock, p20c Zuyeu Uladzimir/Shutterstock, p21 & 31tl K.D. Leperi/Alamy Stock Photo, p22 & 31b JPCarnevalli/Shutterstock, p23 & 30b dpa picture alliance/Alamy Stock Photo, pp24-25 & 31tr Magdanatka/Shutterstock, p26 & 31c ivan canavera/Shutterstock, p27 & 30t Associated Press/Alamy Stock Photo, p28 Martin of Sweden/Shutterstock, p29 Jora Abramov/Shutterstock, p48 Roman Samborskyi/Shutterstock, p49 Yatravel/Shutterstock, p50 Hiro Komae/Alamy Stock Photo, p51 Nynke van Holten/Shutterstock, p52t Vera Larina, p52b Nick Brandt, p53 Danita Delimont/Shutterstock, p54 Roaming Pictures/Shutterstock, p55 scotia26/Alamy Stock Photo, p56t Kolonko/Shutterstock, p56b Jeffrey Isaac Greenberg 9+/Alamy Stock Photo, p57 ZUMA Press, Inc./Alamy Stock Photo.

Published by Collins
An imprint of HarperCollins*Publishers*
The News Building, 1 London Bridge Street, London, SE1 9GF, UK

HarperCollins*Publishers*
Macken House, 39/40 Mayor Street Upper, Dublin 1, D01 C9W8, Ireland

Browse the complete Collins catalogue at
collins.co.uk

'Crater' text © Chris Bradford 2026
All other text, illustrations and design © HarperCollins*Publishers* Limited 2026

Wandle Learning Trust name and logo © Wandle Learning Trust

10 9 8 7 6 5 4 3 2 1

A catalogue record for this publication is available from the British Library.

ISBN 978-0-00-879095-0

All rights reserved. No part of this publication may be reproduced, stored in a retrieval system, or transmitted in any form by any means, electronic, mechanical, photocopying, recording or otherwise, without the prior written permission of the Publisher or a licence permitting restricted copying in the United Kingdom issued by the Copyright Licensing Agency Ltd, 5th Floor, Shackleton House, 4 Battle Bridge Lane, London SE1 2HX.

Without limiting the exclusive rights of any author, contributor or the publisher of this publication, any unauthorised use of this publication to train generative artificial intelligence (AI) technologies is expressly prohibited. HarperCollins also exercise their rights under Article 4(3) of the Digital Single Market Directive 2019/790 and expressly reserve this publication from the text and data mining exception.

Authors: Chris Bradford, Samantha Montgomerie and Joshua Seigal
Illustrators: Jake Hill (Astound US) and Paula Fernández (Astound US)
Publisher: Katie Sergeant
Product manager: Natasha Paul
Education consultant: Charlotte Raby
Project manager: Emily Hooton
Phonics reviewers: Catherine Baker and Abbie Rushton
Proofreader and fact checker: Catherine Dakin
Cover designer: Sarah Finan
Cover illustrator: Paula Fernández (Astound US)
Internal designer: 2Hoots Publishing Services Ltd
Production controller: Sophie Waeland

Developed in collaboration with Wandle Learning Trust

Printed in the UK by Martins the Printers

MIX
Paper | Supporting responsible forestry
FSC
www.fsc.org
FSC™ C013254

Made with responsibly sourced paper and vegetable ink

Scan to see how we are reducing our environmental impact.

Collins would like to thank Abi Rothe, Nicola Dickens and the schools involved in the Code pilot for contributing to the development of this book.

Access the planning and resources to teach this book at littlewandlecode.org.uk